# COCO GRIMES

# MARY STOLZ

# COCO GRIMES

**HarperTrophy**

*A Division of HarperCollins Publishers*

Coco Grimes

Library of Congress Cataloging-in-Publication Data
Stolz, Mary, date
    Coco Grimes / Mary Stolz.
        p.    cm.
    Sequel to : Stealing home.
    Summary: Eleven-year-old Thomas talks his grandfather into driving all
the way across Florida to meet Coco Grimes, an old man who remembers
Negro League baseball, but the actual encounter proves to be bittersweet.
    ISBN 0-06-024232-9. — ISBN 0-06-024233-7 (lib. bdg.)
    ISBN 0-06-440512-5 (pbk.)
    [1. Baseball—Fiction.    2. Negro Leagues—Fiction.    3. Afro-Americans—
Fiction.    4. Grandfathers—Fiction.    5. Florida—Fiction.]    I. Title.
PZ7.S875854Co    1994                                                    93-34153
[Fic]—dc20                                                                    CIP
                                                                              AC

Typography by Steve Scott
❖
First Harper Trophy edition, 1996.

To Sandy Taylor,
her own self
—M.S.

# Chapter ONE

It was the eighth of March, the day before Thomas's birthday.

Grandfather said at breakfast, "If I am not mistaken, Thomas, kings and queens and such unlikely folk often celebrate their birthdays for up to a week. We are going to have a two-day jubilee for yours."

"No kidding?" Thomas said happily. "How?"

"Tomorrow's the party, but today you and I are going to St. Pete—"

"To see the Pirates!" Thomas shouted.

"Right. They're playing the Mets, so we'll get to see Bobby Bonilla."

"*If* he's in the lineup," Thomas said, sounding a trifle glum. Bobby Bonilla, Thomas's longtime hero, was no longer playing for the Pirates, his and Grandfather's longtime best team.

But Thomas cheered up in no time. Baseball was baseball, and the weeks of spring training were the only time that he and Grandfather got to see Major League games. They went as often as they could.

"When're we leaving?" he asked.

"Right now. Have to give the truck plenty of time to understand what's being asked of it."

"I'll get my glove."

Ringo, Thomas's big white cat, followed them to the back porch.

"Going to a ballgame, Ringo. Back by suppertime," Thomas said, stroking the cat's head. He believed that animals appreciated such explanations, and Grandfather agreed.

"Too bad they aren't playing in Bradenton," Thomas said as Grandfather coaxed the pickup to a drowsy start.

The New York Mets did their spring training games at Al Lang Stadium in St. Petersburg. The Pittsburgh Pirates trained at McKechnie Field in Bradenton, a town closer to home, and therefore kinder to their aged truck. "If we ask too much of it," Grandfather sometimes said, "it throws its fenders in the air and breaks down crying."

But today everything was smooth as could be. The pickup behaved itself until the very end of the trip home, a springtime sun shone all day, the hot dogs and Coke tasted the way hot dogs and Coke at a ballpark should, and Bobby-Bo was in the lineup. He went 2 for 4, but just the same the Pirates won, 5–zip.

And a miracle happened.

Thomas and Grandfather were sitting in the left field bleachers, score cards and pencils ready, watching the pregame activity that they enjoyed as much as the game itself. In the batting cage players took turns swatting long fly balls. Others ran wind sprints on the warning track. Coaches hit fungoes to outfielders, infielders threw hard strikes around the horn. Music, noisy and tinny, came from the loudspeakers. In the stands, fans cheered favorite players and booed those currently out of favor. These latter, of course, could get back in with a single swing of the bat.

Some seats behind home plate were occupied by scouts from the Majors. Thomas eyed these powerful men with awe. They had speed guns, and clipboards for making notes. Some, up to date, had laptop computers. With careful, assessing eyes they studied the moves of rookies desperately hoping for a chance at the big time. They watched aging (in their thirties) veterans desperately hoping for another year or two. They watched players certain to be going north when the season started, who'd be aging veterans themselves one day, desperately hoping for one last chance.

Thomas leaned forward, punched his fist in his fielder's glove, hoping, as always, to catch a foul ball that make the seats. Besides, lots of times bullpen guys would take a ball that had dropped into foul territory and toss it into the stands. Thomas remained ready for when that time came. If it ever did. Which it might. *Maybe* it might. It hadn't yet, but as his grandfather often said, "Who knows tomorrow?"

The miracle happened in the fifth inning, when Bobby Bonilla hit a line drive that hooked foul into the bleachers. Glove up, Thomas sprang the moment he realized the ball was actually coming his way. He almost—*almost*—got his mitt on it. But it went over his head, into the hand of a man sitting right behind them.

Thomas, with a catch in his throat—it had come so close, so close!—looked around. "Swell catch," he said, trying hard to smile.

The man tossed the ball up and caught it a couple of times. Then he reached over and dropped it in Thomas's lap!

"Happy birthday, son," he said with a big smile.

"I still can't *believe* it," Thomas said when they were driving home. He kept turning the ball around, digging at the seams with his fingernails, *squeezing* it, to be sure it was really right there in his hand. In his room, he had a ball that Bobby Bonilla had *signed* for him during spring training the year before. Now, not signed, but definitely a Bobby ball, here was another. "I mean, Grandfather—what a wonderful thing for a person to *do*!"

"Well, as he told you—he'd heard us talking about your birthday, then he saw you leap like a good glove man and nearly make the catch. I think he was as happy to give it away as to catch it in the first place."

Thomas studied every scratch and smudge on the ball. "I'll treasure it," he said. "Even if Bobby isn't a Pirate anymore."

"Of course you will. He's a fine ballplayer, no matter where he's playing. Anyway, Pittsburgh will do all right without him, *and* without the rest of the fellows who've gone elsewhere. The fact is, Thomas, no one person is indispensable to a team. May take a year or two, but the Bucs'll come around and be as good as ever."

"I guess," Thomas said, wanting to be convinced.

As they turned off the Tamiami Trail for home, the pickup began to cough.

"Come on, Old Paint," Grandfather wheedled. "Just a couple of miles more and you can have a nice long snooze in your stable. You can do that, can't you?"

It seemed it could, just. Wheezing into the driveway, the engine gave a sputter and a shudder and then went dead.

"Well, I'll give it a going-over in the morning," said Grandfather, who was good with cars. "Let's hope it just needs a rest. All the way to St. Pete and back was asking a lot of it."

After supper, they got the house ready for guests, though they were planning to have the party itself in the backyard.

Thomas dusted furniture, watered the Boston fern, and put all their games away except for a half-completed jigsaw puzzle. He made a bet with himself. When Aunt Linzy came over tomorrow she would either finish it without asking, or she'd ask and then finish it anyway. Grandfather said that jigsaw puzzles were like a drug with her. She just could not resist them.

He collected a week's newspapers that were scattered around Grandfather's chair and tied them for recycling, then cleaned the bathroom and got out fresh linen for his bed. He'd change the sheets first thing in the morning. When Aunt Linzy and Mr. McCallam stayed overnight, Grandfather used the cot in his room, giving his friend the proper bed, and Thomas spent the night on the living room sofa. Aunt Linzy used Thomas's room, which she always called hers. There'd been a time, when Aunt Linzy had stayed with them for several months, that Thomas had minded that. A lot. Now it was just part of the visit.

Thomas looked around the room. Then he went out to the yard, cut some oleander blossoms, and put them in a jar on his bedside table. And that, he said to himself, is *that*.

Satisfied, he went into the kitchen, where Grandfather was preparing a baked bean casserole that would simmer in savory splendor all night in the oven.

"Anything I can do, Grandfather?"

"There certainly is. Take the basket and get a load of vegetables before it gets dark."

"Okay. What do you want?"

"Something of everything would be a good idea."

Thomas, Ringo at his heels, walked down the garden rows, selecting ingredients for the stew.

"This enough?" he asked, setting the big twig basket on the kitchen table.

Grandfather peered in and nodded. "I suppose we could start cutting and chopping now. But I think we've done enough for one day. I'll get up early to start the bread and the casserole."

Grandfather walked to the kitchen window. Thomas joined him, and they watched the sun slowly descending behind a smokey-gray wall of clouds.

"I wonder, Thomas, if we should count on having your party in the backyard after all."

"It's going to rain, isn't it?"

"Looks as if. We'll wait till morning to decide if it's in or out. Either way, it'll be fine, just fine."

"It's gonna be a pretty big party, isn't it?" Thomas counted the guests on his fingers. "Eight people, if we include the Prices' baby girl. They're bringing her."

"Then let's do include her. You might even give her a name."

Thomas shrugged. "Donny told me, but I forget. He usually just says 'the baby' cries a lot."

"Imagine that," said Grandfather, smiling.

"Mr. and Mrs. Price have to walk her up

and down for hours every night. It's a real pain, Donny says."

"No doubt. Some babies have colic—an even bigger pain for them, wouldn't you say?"

"I suppose."

"You cried a lot, as a baby."

"I did? Boy, I bet you didn't like that."

"I didn't mind. I was sorry for you."

"You didn't mind having to listen to me? Honest?"

"Honest."

"Did you have to walk up and down with me at night?"

"No, Thomas," Grandfather said gently. "Your mother and father did that. By the time they—by the time you came to me—you were over colic."

"So why was I crying? After I got to you, I mean?"

"It's difficult to figure what ails a being that can't talk to you. Usually I managed to come up with some sort of comfort, and after a while you'd stop."

"That must've been a relief."

"For both of us."

Thomas's mother, who'd been Grandfather's daughter, and Thomas's father had been killed in an auto accident when he was only a year old. Thomas had come here to live with Grandfather, and here he had been ever since.

He had a picture of his parents on his dresser. Sometimes he thought about them, wished different things about them. But he couldn't remember them. And he could not imagine living with *anyone*—not even that sweet-looking young couple in the picture—except his own grandfather.

# Chapter TWO

**T**he next day it poured.

Thomas stood at the kitchen window, tossing his baseball from hand to hand, and gazed at the dripping trees and bushes, the puddling birdbath, the flooded yard. Rain clinked and clattered on the tin porch roof and flowed through a downspout into a barrel Grandfather used for conserving water.

"This's awful," he said, not turning. "All this rain on my *real* birthday."

"Yes, but suppose it had rained yesterday instead of today?"

Thomas whirled. "Oh, no! That would've been even more *awful*."

"So. Better rain today than yesterday. *That's* how to look at it."

Now that he thought about it, Thomas decided there really was a bright side to this gray wet day. It was cozy, being together, just him,

Grandfather, and Ringo in their kitchen with its clusters of vegetables on the white pine table and marvelous odors wafting from the stove.

"Mr. McCallam says one day you'll be punished for always looking on the bright side of everything."

"Did he now," Grandfather said calmly.

Unperturbed by rain or Mr. McCallam's predictions, Grandfather continued to chop carrots, Florida onions, collard greens, a Seminole pumpkin, string beans, field peas, tomatoes, tiny potatoes, red and yellow and green sweet peppers. The sweet peppers all tasted alike, but Grandfather liked plenty of color in what he cooked. Then he combined the vegetables with elbow macaroni, raisins, toasted walnuts, and a rich brown stock that he always had on hand. Grandfather was preparing a meatless chowder.

Except for Grandfather, Mr. McCallam, Thomas, and Ringo, everyone who was going to be at the party was a vegetarian.

Thomas lifted the lid from the crock of baked beans that was now at the back of the stove, along with two big loaves of Grandfather's homemade bread set there to rise. One wheat, one rye. Closing his eyes, he leaned over to sniff. He could smell better with his eyes shut.

"How're we gonna set things up?" he asked, replacing the lid.

"After I get this chowder on, I'll start the cake—" At Thomas's blissful smile, Grandfather added, "You are to remain in your room while I do that, or go over to Donny's if the rain lets up. The cake is to be a surprise."

"Sure," Thomas said happily. "When should I go?"

"Not yet. First, will you please put the leaf in the living room table, and eight chairs around it—I imagine the baby will bring her own highchair, yes? We'll use the blue tablecloth, and the brown ceramic bowls, and sauce dishes for the baked beans. Tumblers for cider or water. Big spoons. No butter—we can dip bread in the chowder broth. Cloth napkins. Forks for the cake. Oh, yes—did you remember to put flowers in your Aunt Linzy's room?"

"Yeah. Oleanders. Pink and white. And it's my room."

"Now, Thomas."

"I'm only saying . . . I really don't mind, especially."

Grandfather dumped chopped tomatoes into the big iron kettle he'd had as long as Thomas could remember, picked up a wooden spoon and stirred slowly. "I thought I'd make a buffet arrangement in here on the kitchen table, and people can help themselves and carry their bowls into the living room. We'll have a jug of cider and a basket of bread at each end. How's that sound?"

"It sounds *wonderful*."

"Good."

Setting the table, Thomas wondered if he'd ever be like his grandfather. The way he was patient about everything. About everybody.

Take Aunt Linzy. She was the sister of Marta, Grandfather's wife, who had died a long time ago. Aunt Linzy and Grandfather, after not speaking for about forty years, had met again last year when she came from Chicago to Florida and moved right in with them. Without warning, without asking, *she just came and camped and wouldn't leave.*

It had been, for Thomas, for a long while, just awful. She took his room from him, took Ringo's love from him, seemed somehow to take his whole world from him, bossing and finding fault with everything: the way he and Grandfather kept house, the hours they spent listening to baseball games, the fact that they loved to fish. Practically their whole way of *living* was wrong, according to Aunt Linzy, and she'd set about trying to change it.

Then, somehow, living with her had become not so bad, in some ways really all right. Aunt Linzy and Thomas started to understand each other better. Maybe the passage of time had done it. Maybe it had also been Grandfather's gentle resistance to her bossy ways. He listened thoughtfully to everything she said, and then did as he wished. Slowly, without noticing, Thomas had settled for having his great-aunt *live* with them, not just visit.

And then lo! Grandfather's friend Mr. McCallam offered her a job as manager of his motel near Miami and off she'd gone, taking Ivan the Terrible with her. Ivan was a very unpleasant Muscovy duck that had followed Ringo home ages ago. Ivan had liked Ringo, hated Thomas and Grandfather, and had fallen in love on sight with Aunt Linzy.

The funny part was that after she'd gone Thomas sort of missed her. Not enough to want her back living with them, but he found he liked her occasional visits and, no matter what he said, didn't *really* mind if she called his room her room.

By the time Grandfather was ready to start on Thomas's birthday cake, the rain had let up, leaving the backyard a shallow pond of grass and sand. Choruses of birdsong, close by, far off, greeted the sunlight as it glistened on drenched trees and bushes. Rain lilies, under the great live oak, opened their streaky violet cups.

When Thomas came out the back door on his way to Donny's, he drew a startled breath. "Grandfather!" he called. "Come here quick! Lookit!"

In a half-circle of tremendous height, a

double rainbow arched over the Gulf of Mex-ico, each end squarely meeting the water.

"That just about never happens, does it?" said Thomas. "*Both* sides going into the gulf like that. It's perfect, isn't it?"

"Oh yes. Quite perfect."

They stood watching for several minutes before Grandfather went back in the kitchen and Thomas continued on his way to Donny's.

Hours later the company was sitting at the table, blinking contentedly.

"*What* a meal," said Mr. McCallam. "If you ever want a job, Joe, you can hire out as a chef anywhere in the world."

"Oh, now, Milo. You go too far," said Grandfather. He tried to look modest as the Prices and Aunt Linzy joined in the praise. Even the Price baby—her name was Georgia—began to beat on her highchair tray with a spoon.

Thomas, both longing to see his cake and happily aware of a pile of gift-wrapped bundles piled at the other end of the living room, said, "I'll clear the dishes, Grandfather."

Mrs. Price stood. "Oh, no you won't. It's your birthday, Thomas. You are not to lift a finger."

"Not even to open my *presents*?"

"Well, that, of course," said Grandfather. "But first—the moment of the Cake has arrived!"

With everyone except Thomas and Georgia lending a hand, the table was quickly cleared.

Grandfather went into the kitchen, saying over his shoulder, "Eyes shut, please," and returned in a moment. "All right, all, you may look."

"Oh well," said Mr. McCallam. "Now you've outdone yourself. You'll never be able to follow up on this."

There on an old, beautiful cake plate that was one of the earliest things Thomas could remember, was a cake at least six inches high, with a wrap-around cloak of stiff bitter chocolate. Neatly clustered fresh raspberries nestled on whipped cream were encircled by eleven white candles alight.

"Oh MY," said Thomas, beaming.

"A work of art," said Aunt Linzy and Mrs. Price together. Mr. Price rubbed his hands together and his face broke into a broad smile.

"Blow out the candles, Thomas!" Donny urged. "Let's see what's inside."

"I've always considered the blowing out of birthday candles to be highly unsanitary," said Aunt Linzy, but no one paid attention to that as Thomas got all his candles in one breath.

"Did you make a wish?" Donny demanded.

"Sure, and I'm not going to tell."

He had wished that all his life everything would be as wonderful as this birthday, yesterday and today, had been. It's my wish, he said to himself, so I can make it something impossible if I want to.

The inside of the cake proved to be chocolate with apricot butter filling between the layers—all seven of them. And there was Grandfather's homemade ice cream to go with it. "Just a simple vanilla," he said. "Wouldn't want to overdo."

"Of course not," said Mr. McCallam. "As it is, I'm not sure I can make it over to that pile of presents."

From Donny, Thomas got a cassette of Charlie Parker on sax. From Grandfather, a new baseball encyclopedia and a Pirates jacket. A skateboard from Mr. McCallam, because he'd run the old one into the ground. Mrs. Price had knitted him a heavy sweater that he'd be able to wear next winter on days when it got cold, and it got cold in Florida in a way that people who didn't live here wouldn't believe. Mr. Price gave him a book, *Black Diamonds*, by John B. Holway. It was about the Negro League teams that had barnstormed the country back in the days before black players were allowed in the Majors. That was hard to imagine, but true.

"Gee, thanks, Mr. Price. I bet plenty of those guys played as good as anyone who *was* in the Majors."

"You can bet the farm on that, Thomas. Black and white teams used to play one another after the regular season in this country, and in Cuba and Mexico. It is a *documented* fact that of those games, the black teams won more than sixty percent."

"Wow!"

"You'll read about it, and them, in the book. Wonderful book," said Mr. Price, who was an Atlanta Braves fan but at least still in the National League. Grandfather and Thomas were unswerving National League fans.

After the Prices had gone home, Aunt Linzy said she thought she'd retire to her room. On the way, she glanced at the unfinished jigsaw puzzle, stopped, picked up a piece, leaned forward and tucked it in the proper place. She moved away, turned back. One hand to her mouth, she studied the game, then absent-mindedly pulled a chair up to the table and went to work.

Thomas smiled. He had won the bet. He went out on the porch where Mr. McCallam and Grandfather were watching the sun go down. Ringo settled on the railing, studying a great blue heron who stood dozily on one leg under the live oak tree. The rain lilies had already closed up, and would only be wakened by another shower.

Thomas sat on the porch swing, pushing idly back and forth, feeling lazy and replete, like the heron.

Grandfather let out a long contented sigh. "I love these volumptuous southern nights." Thomas laughed.

"*Volumptuous?*" said Mr. McCallam. "Where'd you find that word?"

"In my head. Got a deal of words in my head that aren't in the dictionary."

"I've noticed. Actually—it sounds just right for a night like this." Thomas thought so too.

They listened for a while to the volumptuous night sounds, and then Mr. McCallam said, "That book Frank Price gave you, Thomas, reminded me . . . there's a fellow lives down the street from the motel who 'had a cup of coffee and cookie in the Bigs'—or at the Show—however the expression goes. Way back when. Talks as if those were the glory days, even if he never got anywhere to speak of, himself."

Thomas, alert at once, sat up. "When was *when*?"

"Way back, way back. In the days of the Negro Leagues, that the book's about. He's old. Very old. And cranky."

"Who'd he play for?"

"He mentioned being with the Birmingham Black Barons—I couldn't forget a name like that—and then, I think, he was with the Kansas City Royals—"

"Monarchs," said Grandfather. "They weren't Royal until they got white. They were the Kansas City Monarchs. Jackie Robinson was playing shortstop for them when Branch Rickey decided to embark on the great and long overdue experiment."

"Where'd this man have the cookie and the cup of coffee?" Thomas asked. "Who with? Was it before or after Jackie?"

Mr. McCallam smiled. "Guess you'll just have to drive over and talk to him yourself, right? How about it, Joe?"

"Not on your tintype," said Grandfather. "No way you're going to get me to leave here and drive all the way to Miami on a wild ball chase—"

"Please, Grandfather! Can't we go?"

"Well, *I* think for Thomas's sake you should do it," said Mr. McCallam. "And you'd finally get to see the way my establishment looks now, which I should think you'd have done ages ago."

"If you hadn't chosen to locate it so far away, I *would* have seen it ages ago. It isn't my fault you're at the other end of the state."

"Joe! It's the other coast of Florida, not of the United States. Two hundred easy miles."

"That pickup of ours would expire at the prospect. She wouldn't make it to I-75."

"You're hopeless, you know that? I told Thomas, you're a couple of barnacles, the pair of you. Immovable objects. Sessile creatures. *Hopeless!*"

"I'm not a barnacle," Thomas began. "I'd *love* to drive over and see—"

"Willie Mays's father, Willie Mays, Senior, played for the Birmingham Barons," Grandfather interrupted dreamily. "And Satch did, and Jimmy Crutchfield. Wasn't much of a team, and they all moved on. Except Mr. Mays Senior. He was too old by then, but Willie himself was with them for a spell. It was his first team, before he went up to the Giants. Stopped for a second at a Triple A team. Can't remember which—"

"You *can't?*" Mr. McCallam exclaimed,

winking at Thomas.

"Those old-timers," Grandfather went on in a low, lazy voice, "they played all positions. A man would pitch one end of a double-header, then turn around and catch the second game. Double Duty Radcliffe did it all the time. Infield, outfield—they'd go wherever there was a hole. And some of those ballparks, if that's what you could call them, were nothing but cow pastures. But oh, how those fellows played! Sometimes three games in a day, doubleheader in one town, twi-nighter in another town after a bus ride—"

"And that was supposed to be *fun?*" Mr. McCallam said, shaking his head.

"From what I hear, they loved it," said Grandfather, yawning and getting to his feet. "Me, I'd have given my eye teeth to play anywhere, on any team, in any league, white, black, or phosphorescent."

"Why didn't you?" asked Thomas. He knew that as a boy, Grandfather had been a shortstop with the Zion Baptist Church.

"Seems no one wanted my eye teeth, Thomas. If you'll both excuse me, I'm off to bed."

"Joe! What about my suggestion?" Milo

McCallam said.

"What suggestion was that?"

"You know darn well. What about you and Thomas driving over to see me?"

"Oh, that suggestion." Grandfather waved his hand. "Out of the question."

After the screen door had closed, and Ringo had rearranged himself on the porch railing, Thomas said, "This man you know, Mr. McCallam—what's his name? Maybe he's in my baseball encyclopedia."

"I doubt it. He's called Coco Grimes. I guess the Coco is one of those wonderful nick-names they all got, like Double Duty Radcliffe that your grandfather mentioned. I never heard of him, but old Grimes, the couple of times I met him—and he can't talk anything but baseball—spoke of Crush Holloway and Mule Suttles, Welday Walker, Ghost Marcelle—isn't that a great name?—and let's see—well, some others I can't recall."

"You said he's awfully old—"

"In his nineties."

"But he's still *alive*."

"Last I knew, he was. I'm going to bed, Thomas."

"So if we come over, you can get me to meet him?"

"If you can persuade your grandfather to drive all the way to the east coast, you're a better man than I am. I've been after him for *years* to get over for a visit, and he comes up with excuses that a child of four wouldn't credit. Yup, your grandfather will keep you a pair of barnacles stuck to the bottom of the boat."

Settled on the sofa, Ringo beside him, Thomas reached for *Black Diamonds*, and as he did, knocked another book off the table. It was the notebook Aunt Linzy had given him for his birthday. It was bound in smooth red leather and had Thomas's initials stamped in gold on the front cover. Opening it, he'd been puzzled to find the pages blank.

"It's a yearly journal," his great-aunt had explained.

"What for?"

"For you to keep."

"How?"

"Thomas. You must know what a journal is."

"Well, I don't."

"Pshaw," Aunt Linzy said. Grandfather claimed she was the only person he knew who said that. Puh*shaw*, it sounded like.

"At day's end, Thomas, you write your thoughts, or note down what the past day held that seems to you interesting—good or bad. At the end of the year you can reread it and know just what happened and when."

Why would I want to do that? Thomas wondered.

"Seems an interesting idea, Thomas," Grandfather had observed. "Then at the close of each entry, you must write, 'And so to bed.'"

"Why?" said Thomas and Aunt Linzy together.

"Because the great English journal-keeper, Samuel Pepys, closed his entries that way. It's good to follow in the footsteps of illustrious forebears."

"I scarcely *think*," Aunt Linzy said, "that an

English journalist would be a forebear of ours."

"Journal-keeper, not journalist. Anyway, Linzy, I like to think all writers are ancestors and descendants of one another, keepers of knowledge."

"Well. It's a nice thought. In any case, Thomas, I thought you might like to keep a journal. Perhaps you can put it away for when you're older."

Now, on impulse, Thomas took the red leather notebook, got a pencil from the desk drawer, and began to write.

*This was a great birthday, and yesterday was great too. What a cake. Mr. McCallam knows a man who played in the Negro Leagues and knew lots of the old-time guys. I am going to make Grandfather drive over to Miami so I can meet him, his name is Coco Grimes and he is very old so I want to get there before he dies or something. I don't think I'll keep this journal for a whole year but who knows . . .*

He read this, started to close the book, then wrote, *And so to bed . . .*

"Okay, Ringo," he said. "Lights out."

# Chapter THREE

"**N**o!" said Grandfather. "Absolutely not!"

"But why—"

"Because I say so, that's why."

Thomas stared at Grandfather in disbelief. Grandfather rubbed his beard irritably. "Sorry. Of course I don't mean that. But Thomas—you know I don't like to travel. I don't like to leave home. Until now, you've never wanted to, either. We're comfortable here, aren't we?"

"Yes, but—"

"You're always saying you want everything to be the same, nothing ever changed—"

"Yes, but a person can change their *minds*, right? So I've changed mine. I want to meet this old guy who played with Willie Mays's father and the rest of them back then. And I don't think going to Miami is really *traveling*.

Not like we were going to Pittsburgh."

Thomas and Grandfather often spoke of driving north during the season to see the Pirates play at Three Rivers Stadium, but somehow they never got around to it.

"Grandfather, it's different now," he persisted. "Mr. McCallam wants you to see his motel and you never have, and he's your friend, and—"

"I've seen it."

"Years ago," Thomas said. "He wants us to see it *now*."

"And all of a sudden, so do you." Grandfather smiled.

"I *said* it's partly—mostly—because of meeting Mr. Grimes. When'll I ever get a chance like this again, huh? And hey!" Thomas said, inspired, "I could make it an interview, for the school paper. I mean, *that's* a reason all by itself to go over there, isn't it?"

"It would be. And I understand how you feel, whether you think I do or not. But, look, Thomas—taking the pickup clear across Florida, we'd risk being stranded on the roadside for the rest of our lives. Even if we made it, we'd be eating in strange places, sleeping in strange beds—"

Thomas took a deep breath. He stared at the floor and bit his lip. "Okay, Grandfather."

Grandfather sighed. "Oh, Thomas, I'm just trying to make you see that even if we were prepared to undertake a trip, the truck is *not*. Pittsburgh or Miami, those wheels wouldn't make it to either. It barely trundled back from St. Pete."

"Did you try to start it this morning?"

"I did, and it did. I could get out of the driveway, and as far as the market. Probably. Are *you* prepared to set off for the east coast in it?"

Thomas slumped and shook his head. "No, I guess not, Grandfather."

It would have been so wonderful to meet, to talk with, to listen to, a man who had known Willie Mays and Satchel Paige and Cool Papa Bell and who could tell how many other great old-time ballplayers of the olden days he had known and *played* with. But now it wasn't going to happen.

"Thomas," Grandfather said, taking his hand. "I am truly sorry. I'd take you in a minute, if there was some way we could do it. You know that."

Thomas nodded. He did know that. But they both knew their truck was long past such a trip.

Then one day the following week, when Thomas got home from school, Grandfather was there at the door waiting for him.

"Tell me, Thomas, how'd you like to take a trip?" he asked.

"Are you kidding?"

"I don't kid about important matters."

"A trip where?"

"Well now, to Milo's motel on the outskirts of Miami, of course. So that you can meet this holdover from the olden days."

"You *mean* it?"

"Thomas! Would I make the offer if I didn't mean it?"

"No, but what are we going to do—walk?"

Grandfather laughed. "We are going in a real car."

"Where'd we get a real car?"

"Cal Grissom says he'll be happy to lend us one for the weekend, so what do you think of that?"

Thomas let out a shout of joy and threw his arms around Grandfather.

"So that's what happened," he told Donny later. "Grandfather's friend, the one he fishes out on the gulf with, Mr. Grissom, who owns the used car business downtown, said 'For goodness' sakes, Joe, of course you can take one of my heaps for a jaunt to Miami.'"

"That's what he said?"

"Word for word." Thomas sighed happily.

"Your grandfather *asked* him for the loan of a car?"

"I know. I was sorta surprised. I mean, really surprised." Grandfather was not inclined to ask favors. Too proud. "He did it for me, so I could meet Coco Grimes."

"Gosh."

"So we're gonna go this weekend. You can come too, if you want to, Donny. Grandfather says so."

"Oh well, heck, Thomas. This's the weekend we're going to Busch Gardens. I was supposed to ask if *you* wanted to go with us."

"How about that?" Thomas exclaimed. "Everything coming at the same time."

"Well, but you maybe wouldn't have another chance to—I mean, you know, he might die or something," said Donny, echoing Thomas's thought.

"That's what I'm afraid of."

They talked about it some more and decided that Busch Gardens would always be there, whereas a man over ninety might not make it past the weekend.

School was closed on Friday because of a teachers' meeting, so the plan was to leave Friday morning, spend that night and Saturday with Mr. McCallam and Aunt Linzy, then drive back on Sunday. Donny promised to see to it that Ringo got food, water, companionship, and conversation during his three days without Thomas.

"Except for Saturday," he cautioned.

"I know. Busch Gardens."

"But I'll feed him before we leave and after we get back," Donny said.

"And pet him, too," Thomas reminded him.

"Sure thing."

Grandfather and Thomas were taking house gifts. Frozen snook fillets packed in ice for Mr. McCallam, and a jigsaw puzzle they figured even Aunt Linzy couldn't finish in fifteen minutes. It was solid navy blue and black, with more than a thousand pieces. They had their lunch in a Styrofoam picnic box. Grandfather flatly refused to enter a fast-food joint.

Thomas gave Ringo a hug, then Donny and Ringo stood on the front porch to watch them drive away in Mr. Grissom's nice four-door Chevy.

Thomas had never been in such a fine car before. He bounced up and down on the soft seat, twisted to look at where there was a whole backseat all to themselves if they wanted it, turned on the air conditioner and then, at Grandfather's request, turned it off again. According to his grandfather, air conditioners were ripping the ozone layer to bits.

They took I-75 for the first leg of the journey. Grandfather, of course, was obliged to watch the road. Thomas buried himself in *Black Diamonds* and thought about the questions he would ask Coco Grimes, and miles passed without a word exchanged. Grandfather disliked driving, distrusted a strange car no matter how comfortable, and discouraged conversation when he was at the wheel. Still, now and then he'd pull off the road so that they could look at some interesting sight—a mound of chalky clouds in fantastic formation, a banyan tree of tremendous girth and age. For nearly fifteen minutes they watched a bald eagle perched atop a telephone pole. They passed fields where herds of Brahma bulls stood massively still, cotton-white cattle egrets scattered among them, some perched atop their great humps.

Toward noon, Grandfather took a side road and drove till they found a meadow with a low stone wall easily stepped over. In the shade of a water oak, they ate lunch—cheese, wheat crackers, apples, gingersnaps, lemonade from a big thermos.

"Now," said Grandfather. "Isn't this preferable to one of those highway grease spots?"

Thomas, who'd have liked to eat in a "fast-food joint," didn't answer.

On the road again, Thomas fell asleep, and woke only as Grandfather pulled into La Casa de Ladra, Mr. McCallam's motel, a series of one-story cottages painted a soft Spanish pink with white shutters at the windows. Instead of a grass lawn, beach daisies and blue blaze grew low to the ground. White and pink oleanders were lush with blossoms, and everywhere hibiscus bushes were in bloom. Beside a sunny, glittering pool were people, some black, some white, stretched out on canvas lawn chairs. Children leaped in a fountain springing at the shallow end.

"Hey, this's neat!" Thomas said.

"I detect your aunt's touch. Last time I was here the place didn't sparkle this way."

Milo McCallam came running from the office, hands outstretched. "You made it, you made it! I expected a call saying Thomas had measles, or the Pirates had been sold to New

Zealand." He opened his arms wide, gesturing toward his domain. "What do you say, Joe? Place looks great, doesn't it?"

"Palatial. You've done miracles."

"True, true. But I should explain that Linzy's responsible. She got the place painted, all the old furniture thrown out, everything neat and clean and pretty and brand new. And just look around you! Business is *booming*. People drive by, see this place shining here like a prism at the roadside, and in they come like trout on a reel."

Again he swept his arm around with proud possessiveness, then led them down a flower-lined walk to their cottage.

"Where *is* Linzy?" Grandfather asked.

"Seeing to things in the coffee shop, I imagine. We're trying to decide whether to start serving dinner in addition to breakfast and lunch. Be an awfully big move, if we make it. Well, I'll leave you to unpack, then see you in my house. The one at the very end of the walk, as far away as I can get. Linzy's cottage is at the other end of the loop. We're going out to dinner tonight at a great Cuban restaurant in Little Havana. Get a rest first, because we stay up late."

"Me, too?" Thomas asked.

"Sure, you too. Think I'd leave you here with a sitter?" Mr. McCallam said, laughing. He glanced at Grandfather. "Won't do him any harm to stay up all night for a change, will it?"

"All *night?*" Grandfather growled.

"Kidding, Joe. Just kidding. Well—see you. I really am darned glad to have you here. You know that."

He was gone.

The cottage had twin beds with maple head-boards and tufted white bedspreads. White lacy curtains cast intricate afternoon shadows across the tile floor. There were a desk, two comfortable chairs, and an oval rag rug. Thomas thought the bathroom was like the in-side of a lime sherbet—clean and cool and palely green.

"Amazing, what your aunt Linzy can do in the decorating line," Grandfather said.

Over his protests and grumblings, she had made a lot of changes in their own house when she'd lived with them. She'd done most of the work herself, sewing curtains and slip-covers. With Thomas's help she'd painted the house inside and out. When it was all done, even Grandfather had to admit improvement.

"So," Grandfather said now. "We are actually here."

"Are you glad?" Thomas asked.

"I'll answer that after I take a shower and a little snooze."

"Okay. I'm gonna go in that pool."

Returning from his swim, Thomas encountered his aunt Linzy, who greeted him affectionately. "How good to see you," she said, giving him a hug. "We weren't sure you'd actually make it."

"I guess maybe we wouldn't, except Mr. Grissom loaned us one of his cars. Grandfather *asked* him."

"Oh? That was generous. Of your grandfather, I mean. Of course, Mr. Grissom too. But Joe doesn't like asking anything of anybody."

"I know," said Thomas. "He did it for me. So I could meet this man who played in the Negro Leagues practically centuries ago."

"Milo's told me. That must be an exciting prospect for you."

"You know—" Thomas hesitated, then went on. "I'm kinda nervous about it."

"Why?"

"Mr. McCallam says he's sometimes grouchy. Suppose I say the wrong thing?"

"I wouldn't worry about that, Thomas. You're a tactful boy. How is school?"

"It's okay."

"What does that mean?"

"I'm doing pretty good."

"Pretty well."

"That, too."

"How's your arithmetic?"

"About the same."

"That's a shame. Would you like me to tutor you a bit over the weekend?"

"No! I mean, thanks, Aunt Linzy, but I want to just relax. Take it easy, you know."

"Of course. From your many exertions," she said in a dry tone.

He squirmed and looked longingly toward

the cottage where Grandfather was.

"Are you keeping your journal?" she asked.

Thomas answered with some enthusiasm. "It's sort of interesting, doing that."

"I told you, didn't I? I trust you keep it faithfully?"

"Not *faithfully*, but pretty often." Thomas looked about. "Where's Ivan?" he asked. "I haven't seen him yet."

Aunt Linzy shook her head sadly. "He charged the UPS truck. On the side the driver couldn't see."

"Did he get run over?"

"He did. I know he wasn't a very appealing creature, and he behaved more like a guard dog than a duck, but I liked him. I miss him."

"Maybe you could get another duck," Thomas offered, not believing that even Aunt Linzy would want to do that.

"No. There was only one Ivan."

"That's a fact," said Thomas, thinking of all the times Ivan had bitten his ankles or jumped out, hissing at him, from ambush. Yes, there was only one Ivan.

Squirrel-gray clouds were beginning to mound over the ocean, and Thomas shivered, clasping his arms across his chest, hands in his armpits.

"Thomas, you're cold. Run along, now, and I'll see you later."

"Mr. McCallam says we're all going out to dinner—"

"Not I," she said sharply. "I do not spend money on restaurants when I have a perfectly good kitchenette in my cottage. I am not a rich woman, and must eat within my purse. What are you laughing at?"

"I'm not!" Thomas said, trying not to giggle again.

"It's a common expression, Thomas. It means to live within one's means."

Thomas shivered again, overdoing it a bit. "I gotta go get dressed, Aunt Linzy." He started off, turned back, hovered uncertainly. He didn't want to be rude.

"Go, go," she said. "I'll see you in the morning."

At well past midnight, ten people sat around a table in the garden of the Cuban restaurant. It was in a part of Miami that Mr. McCallam said was called "Little Havana" because so many expatriate Cubans lived in the area.

Lanterns swinging from tree branches and kerosene lamps on the table gave the only light. A steel band twangled in the darkness. Everyone was talking at once, somehow contriving to hear and answer what everyone else said.

Thomas decided he'd rather listen and eat than shout.

Platters of fried plantains, of black beans and rice, of saffron shrimp and fried pork were passed back and forth, along with great baguettes of hot crispy bread. The spicy aromas blended with that of strong Cuban coffee, of beer, of Coca-Cola, of lemonade.

Thomas looked around the restaurant, listening happily to all that was going on. If he'd known visiting Mr. McCallam would be like this, he'd have asked Grandfather to come here ages ago, even before he heard about Coco Grimes.

Poor Aunt Linzy. Lookit all she's missing.

"Having a good time, Thomas?" Grandfather inquired.

"It's wonderful! Pass me that shrimp, will you, Grandfather?"

There were all different colors of people at their table, and all ages, including a baby on the lap of a lady named Lourdes. There was a cop sitting next to Thomas. There were also a young white man who was a librarian, and a black fellow who taught school, and their wives. Thomas had given up trying to remember who everybody was.

He did know the cop's name. Pollyanna Welles. She was Mr. McCallam's friend.

Thomas thought Officer Pollyanna Welles was neat. A plainclothes detective, very nice-looking.

"Is it scary?" he had asked her, lifting his voice. "Your job, I mean?"

"It has scary moments. Mostly it's routine. Don't ask if I've ever had to shoot anybody."

"I wasn't going to."

"Sorry. I'm touchy on the subject. Just about *everyone* asks that as soon as they find out what I do."

Now Thomas decided he *would* be interested to know if she'd ever shot anyone, but certainly wasn't going to ask. Instead he said,

"Do you know Mr. Grimes? Coco Grimes, who used to play baseball years and years ago, and got to the Majors in time to be too old for them?"

"I'm not personally acquainted with him, but certainly he's well-known around these parts. Old as the mountains, talkative as a parrot. Grouchy as a parrot sometimes, too, from what I've heard."

"I'm gonna meet him tomorrow, so he can tell me about the game in the olden days. I hope he doesn't feel grouchy."

"You like baseball?"

Thomas thought a moment. "I guess I *love* it. Grandfather, too. Both of us. Do you?"

"Love it? Well, no, Thomas. Does that disqualify me?"

Thomas laughed. "No. We know people who don't, like Mr. McCallam, and we like them anyway. And after I meet Coco Grimes tomorrow, Mr. McCallam says we're going to a raree. What's one like? I've never been to a raree."

"It's a street fair. Have you ever been to one of those?"

"To the county fair a couple of times."

"This is like that, only not so elaborate. But fun."

"Are you going to it?"

"No. I have to work tomorrow, and right now I'm getting sleepy. Good night, Thomas."

"It's nice to meet you."

The detective glanced across the table at Mr. McCallam, who nodded and got up to see her to the door.

Thomas watched them go. I think they like each other, he thought. Then he gave a tremendous yawn. He couldn't remember being up this late ever before.

"Me, too," Grandfather muttered.

"You too, what?" Thomas asked, yawning again.

"Me too, I'm ready for bed. Let's go."

# Chapter FOUR

**D**espite getting to bed at such a late—or, actually, early—hour, Thomas and Grandfather were up at dawn.

"Grandfather?" Thomas said as they dressed, "don't you think this's gonna be too early for me to go to Mr. Grimes's house?"

"Milo told you, it's all been arranged. They're expecting you this early."

"Okay, but what I want to know is why don't you want to meet him, too?"

Grandfather smiled. "I can't go out on the charter boat with Milo *and* spend the morning with an old ballplayer, no matter how interesting that might be."

Mr. McCallam and two of his friends had chartered a deep-sea fishing boat, with a captain, to give Grandfather a chance to go after tarpon. Of course he wouldn't want to miss that, for any reason.

After breakfast in the coffee shop, Thomas and Mr. McCallam set off for the house where Coco Grimes lived with his grandson and family.

They walked along a street of two-story stucco houses. Some looked proud, with trim lawns, flowers, shining windows. Others had broken windows repaired with cardboard, grassless littered front yards, rust stains running from gutters. Skinny cabbage palms lined the sidewalk.

A tingle ran down Thomas's spine. He was this close to meeting a man who had actually known—looked at, talked to, maybe *played* with—Satch and Oscar Charleston and Willie, and Willie's father, and Cool Papa Bell, and who knew how many others that maybe Thomas hadn't even heard of, but should have, except that they had long ago disappeared into the mixed-up jumble of Negro League statistics.

"You're *sure* he knows I'm coming to see him, Mr. McCallam?"

"Thomas, he's going to be very pleased. Not many children—not many people at all—want to listen to an old man's reminiscences. I told his son that you're going to do a piece for your school paper on the meeting, and they're all proud as punch."

"Somebody told me that sometimes he's sort of—grouchy."

"Who isn't—sometimes? And you have to remember that the man is nearly a hundred years old—"

"A hundred!" Thomas gasped. "That's—that's ninety years older than I am!"

"So, if you live another ninety, maybe you'll be a grouch once in a while, too."

Thomas, who was never sure about the age of anyone much past twelve, laughed at the notion of a boy getting to be an old man.

"I did tell you he's in a wheelchair, didn't I?" Mr. McCallam said.

Thomas slowed his steps. "Gee, no. You didn't. That's a shame."

"He had a stroke a few years ago. Before

that he used to walk a couple of miles every day, rain or shine."

Maybe, Thomas thought, being practically a hundred he doesn't mind being in a wheelchair with a stroke and not having to walk every day. Except how could he not mind?

"So now he lives with his grandson, huh?"

"And family. Joe Grimes. He's a telephone repairman, about the size of William Perry."

"Who? Oh, you mean the Fridge. The guy with the Chicago Bears."

"It beats me how a boy can know so much about one game and nothing at all about any other."

"Beats me, too," said Thomas who did, in fact, like basketball, even ice hockey, once in a while. It was Grandfather who considered anything but baseball a waste of time.

The Grimeses' house seemed to Thomas sort of in between proud and run-down. An old bike leaned against the porch, a couple of weather-stained rockers were on the porch, and one banister was missing from the railing. But the stucco was freshly painted, and bright white curtains were at the windows.

Thomas, who had never lived on a street, thought with sudden homesickness of his and Grandfather's small house on the Gulf of Mexico. This was bigger, but theirs was—well, it was *theirs*.

The front door opened, and there, just about filling it, stood the Refrigerator—except he was really someone else—with a great bright smile and a voice like a tuba.

"Hey, hey!" he said, stepping back in the hall and all but scooping them in. "Tom, this's great, just great. Gramps is busting to see you. Got himself all duked up, ready for the interview."

Thomas, still a little nervous, almost protested when Mr. McCallam said, "I'll be getting along, Joe. Time and charter boats wait for no man. You'll be able to find your way back, won't you, Thomas?"

"Uh . . . sure. Sure, I can," Thomas said as Mr. McCallam went down the stairs and away.

"Come on, Tom," said Joe Grimes. "You're skittish about this, right?"

"Well—"

"Don't be. Gramps is just an old man who lived for baseball. Nothing to be afraid of." A big hand rested on Thomas's shoulder. "He'd be disappointed, you know, if you changed your mind now."

"I just—got a little—" He bit his lip. "I mean, Mr. Grimes—meeting somebody that knew all those guys . . ."

"I know. Believe me, he's dying to tell you all about it. But don't believe *everything* he says."

"Huh?"

"He's going on a hundred, and had a stroke a couple of years back."

"Mr. McCallam told me."

"Most of the time he's fine. But he does mix things up. Times, dates, people." Joe Grimes gave a deep laugh. "I should talk. Half the time my brain is just a bowl of pebbles. Anyway, just expect him to get a bit muddled once in a while. For his age, he's got it pretty together. And don't take anything personally if he gets cranky about how the world's gone to pot, especially where baseball's concerned. It's his theme song. *Then* was great—even though it wasn't, you know. And *now* is terrible, which in some ways it is and in other ways a long long way from what he put up with in his day."

"What position did he play?"

"Caught, mostly. But they didn't only switch hit in those days. They switched positions from one game to the next. The only thing he never did was pitch, and he always envied the hurlers. Got in a fistfight with Satchel Paige once."

"No *kidding*!"

"Sure enough. Satch hit him with an inside slider, and poor old Gramps—wasn't old then, of course—charged the mound."

Thomas's mouth fell open.

"*Nobody* charged the mound when Satchel Paige was on it. No*body*," said Joe Grimes.

"But *he* did?"

"Just that once, believe me. Satch was one big strong fellow, and Gramps was kind of a peewee. He came to in the dugout, with all the fellows laughing at him. He still holds it against LeRoy."

Thomas knew that Satch's real name had been LeRoy. But *imagine* it—he was going to talk to a man who'd been knocked out by Satchel Paige. Wait'll he told Donny!

"Did you ever play, Mr. Grimes?"

"Softball. Still do. Weekends for the Zion Baptists. That's my church. We have a pretty good team."

Thomas wondered if they were all as big as Joe Grimes.

"My grandfather once played for the Zion Baptists, and his name is Joe, too," Thomas said. "Isn't that a coincidence?"

"Sure is. Gramps is Joe, too. But he's been Coco since he played for the Barons. They all got nicknames in those days."

"I know. I've been reading about it in this book I've got."

"Is that so? Well—let's not keep him waiting. Tom—remember if he gets a bit touchy, it's nothing personal, and it doesn't last. You'll understand, okay?"

"Sure, Mr. Grimes."

"Call me Joe."

They went down the hall to the kitchen, where

Mr. Coco Grimes, wearing a crisp blue-and-white–striped shirt and khaki pants, was sitting erect in his wheelchair, right hand lying in his lap, fingers curled upward. He looked at Thomas with clouded brown eyes and a happy, nearly toothless smile of greeting.

"Granddad, here's Tom Weaver, a great fan of yours."

Mr. Grimes extended a twiggy left hand. "Ever see me play, son? I caught for the Cleveland Indians. Guess you know about that, all right. You ever catch me when I was catching?" He waved his left hand merrily at the joke, clearly one he'd used before.

Thomas walked over and grasped the hand of the old southpaw. "Guess not, sir. It's just that I've heard so much about you, and I thought—I thought it'd be fun if we could talk."

"Course it'll be fun. Barrel of monkeys. Joe, how 'bout takin' me out t' the yard. This young feller and I'll have our conversation in the fresh air."

"Sure thing, Gramps," said Joe Grimes. He picked up the wheelchair, Coco and all, and walked to the kitchen door. "Open up, Tom," he said, not even breathing hard.

They went down a few steps to the back-yard, where a slim lady in jeans and an old shirt was weeding a border garden of petunias and geraniums.

"This is my wife, Tom. And here's Tom Weaver, Marylou," Joe said, still holding the wheelchair as if it were a basket of balloons.

Mrs. Grimes put down her trowel, removed her gardening gloves, and came to take Thomas's hand.

"At last! Gramps is so pleased to be meeting someone who is interested in his *helden* days."

"Helden?"

"Sorry. I teach German and tend to take it home with me. *Helden* means hero. For Gramps, those were the heroic days, even if some of us would disagree with him."

Joe deposited his grandfather in the shade of a huge live oak tree. Its twisted branches were draped with trailing wisps of Spanish moss, and beneath it, obviously never moved, was a wooden table, weatherworn and, Thomas was pretty sure, handmade.

"I'll go in and rustle up some cookies and lemonade, while you two have your talk," said Mrs. Grimes.

"Mr. Grimes," said Thomas, "is it okay with you if I write about our talk for our school paper?"

"I'm proud to be in your paper, all right—but my name's Coco, sonny. Mr. Grimes was my father. After he got free. He was a slave. You people today don't have any *idea* what us people put up with, back then. Not that *I* was a slave, but I know what went on, know every least and last thing about it, don't think I don't."

Joe Grimes brought over another chair. "Sit close to him, Tom. He's a bit deaf, so don't mumble, okay? He really is awfully glad to have company, I know you'll understand, if he—you know—gets a mite touchy," he said again.

For a moment Thomas and the old man studied each other, then both began to speak at once.

"You first," Thomas said, laughing.

"No, no. What was you gonna say? Ask me questions. That's how interviews go on the TV. One person asks the questions and the other person gives out with the answers." The ancient voice was hoarse, wavery, hesitant.

But he knows what he wants to say, Thomas thought.

He leaned forward and tried to speak loud enough. "I just thought, sir, that you could tell me about your days in the old-time leagues, the Negro Leagues."

"Don't shout. And don't say *sir*. The name's Coco. Coco Grimes, catcher for the Tribe, the Cleveland Indians. See you keep that in mind, sonny."

"I will." Thomas bit his lip, thinking that Mr. Coco Grimes was getting down to the "touchy" part pretty fast. He started over.

"Somebody said you played with the Birmingham Black Barons. Is that right, Coco?"

"And the Philadelphia Stars, the Homestead Grays, and—lessee—the Baltimore Elite Giants. I was with a mort of teams before they called me up to Cleveland."

"Were you always behind the plate?"

"Heck, no. We played wherever there was a hole. We all did. Guy'd pitch a game, catch the next one, travel to another town, cover center, or right. Left. Short. Wherever.

I had a good arm from anywhere."

Thomas had just read about this way of playing, and heard about it from Mr. Price and Grandfather. But it was different hearing it from a person who had *been* there, had *played* then, with those old-time heroes.

"Mostly I caught," the old man went on. "Played with Josh Gibson, that was with the Homestead Grays. What a team that was! Smokey Joe Williams, Lefty Williams pitching. And Josh. Can't say enough about Josh. He was my friend, you know. Roomed together for one season, we did. Greatest catcher there ever was. And hit! One year he belted seventy-two home runs."

"*Seventy-two!*" Thomas said. "Wow!"

"You heard me. Seventy-two. You can look it up. That was with the Homestead Grays, back in twenty-nine, maybe it was thirty. You remember that time he sent a ball clear out of Yankee Stadium? Fair ball. That was the days when black and white teams barnstormed all over the country, playing each other, and in Mexico and Cuba and Puerto Rico, all those places, after the regl'r season, to make a bit extra money. Babe Ruth never hit a ball right outta Yankee Stadium, no sir. You heard about that feat by Gibson? Ever see him at the plate? Or behind it, fer the matter of that. He could throw a man out from his knees. You ever see that? Better catcher than me, by gosh, Josh."

"I didn't see him. But my grandfather tells me lots about the—"

"Went by bus. Sometimes play three games in a day. Two games in one town, drive to another, play a twi-nighter, but those got called on account o' darkness lots of times—only time a game'd end in a tie. Until they started carrying around these here portable lights, then we played night games, too. Think it was the Homestead Grays first did that with lights—like a bunch of candles at first. It was a mess, pitcher couldn't pick up the signals, I'd call for one down and in, get it high and tight, mebbe on the noggin. Now they got these lights, you'd think it was noontime at midnight. Not then. Now they ride around in airplanes, get these godawful salaries like kings. Guys make big money that never get off the bench. We was lucky to get paid at all. Rode in the bus, ate in it, changed in it. Fifty cents a day meal money, sometimes a dollar. Stop in some town for food, but couldn't go in and sit down at the tables. Went 'round to the back door, got sandwiches, soda pop, in paper bags, go back in the bus to eat. Slept in it, too. Some fellows didn't have no trouble sleepin' in the bus, but I just never could—rickety they were, and the roads no good back then. No way to treat human beings."

"No. No, it was no way—" Thomas started to agree.

"Later on, you know, *we*—us black fellas— got into organized ball, the Majors, not that we didn't have our own leagues, as major and good as theirs anyday, sometimes better, only a man don't like bein' *kept out.* I'da been happy to play with my own kind forever, but not when I was bein' *kept outta theirs.* Tell the truth, there wasn't a spit's difference between our leagues and the so-called Majors, playing-wise. Now—lemme see—who was it brought up the first black player to the white Majors—Branch Water? Was that the name?"

"Branch Rickey."

"If you say so. He went'n got a fellow was playin' shortstop for the Monarchs, Jackie

Robinson. First he went up to Montreal, then to Brooklyn, that Ebbetts Field that's no longer there. Jackie broke the barrier—remember in the Bible how Joshua fit the battle of Jericho and the walls come tumblin' down? That's what Jackie did—sent the walls tumblin' down, but lemme tell you, there was fellows as good shoulda got there before. Just the same, he was one tough fellow. Put up with a lot of—well, won't say the word in front of a little boy." Mr. Grimes stopped for breath, blinked and looked about him, frowning. "What was I saying?"

"You were telling about Jackie Robinson."

"Right, that's right. What that fella put up with, I just clean don't know how he did it. It was cruel, plain cruel. Not just the dad-blamed fans, but his own *teammates*, by which I mean fellows who were playing on the same team, but not what you'd call *mates*. There was one fellow Jackie said was decent to him, right from the start. Pee-wee—something."

"Pee-wee Reese."

"Right. O'course, once they caught on to how he was gonna take them right to the top—he was playin' second by then—they began bein' nice, sorta. And then along comes Larry Doby and Campy and Newcombe and those guys and now we're on every team all over, but it was tough in the beginning. But thing is—we were tough, too. We'd been through it *all*."

He sighed into silence, and Thomas was wondering if he should wait, or leave, when Mrs. Grimes came down the back steps.

"Lemonade and chocolate chips," she said, putting a tray on the table. She poured Thomas a glassful, then, filling the other halfway, said, "Here you are, Gramps. Nice and sweet, the way you like it." She sat on the grass beside Thomas's chair. He started to get up, but she patted him back. "I'm fine on the ground. Okay if I listen?"

"Oh, yes," said Thomas, and added, "maybe I'm getting him tired? I wouldn't want to—"

"I'm not tired! I just took a little time out. And I'm not deaf."

"Okay!" Thomas almost snapped, caught himself and added, "I mean, I'm glad you aren't tired."

"You talk about Ty Cobb—"

Thomas was bewildered. These loping strides around the bases of the past were confusing, and half the time Coco seemed to think he was talking to somebody who'd *played* back then. But he tried to look as if he knew all about these players, and that seemed sufficient for the old man to go on.

Mrs. Grimes touched Thomas's knee reassuringly.

"Lemme tell you—they say this here Cobb was this great hitter. Well, Josh Gibson coulda left him standing at the plate like a drugstore Injun. They say Cobb stole bases like a second-story man? Cool Papa Bell could spot him a base and still get home in front of him. Oh, Cool Papa! He could hit all right, but sometimes, just fer the fun of it, he'd drop a bunt'n be on first before the bat hit the ground. You interested in some o' the other old-timers?"

"Well, maybe Satch—" Thomas said without thinking.

Coco scowled. "It's a cryin' shame!" he said, trying to lift his frail voice. "You'd think there wasn't nobody else ever throwed a ball but that there Satchel *Paige*. Oh, he was *good*, real real good, *and* showy as a rooster in a circus parade. But lemme tell you this—on his best day he couldn'ta matched Smokey Joe Williams—you ever see Smokey Joe? Hurled for the Homestead Grays, Bacharach Giants, American Giants—back there in the twenties, into the thirties. You ever see *him*, I'm askin'?"

"No, sir. I mean, no I never did, Coco."

"One year Smokey Joe won forty-one and lost but *three*. Hear that? That's what we was like back then. These days, a man hurls twenty games, they give him that Cy Young award. It was *nothin'* for our fellas to win over thirty games. *And* go the distance. Whatcha got now? Starters hurl a few innings, out comes the hook, then you got this long relief fer mebbe two-thirds of a inning—hook again. Here come yer *short* relief. Hook. Now the danged *table-setters*. Table-setters! What's that mean, anyways, table-setters? Then what happens? In comes yer saver'n the way they play these days, you still gotta have a *closer* primed'n ready t' come out'n lose the danged game—"

Coco struggled with his good hand to get a handkerchief from his pocket. Thomas resisted the urge to help since Mrs. Grimes made no move to. Coco blew his nose, put the handkerchief on his lap. "You know I caught fer the Indians? Did I tell you that yet? Cleveland Indians. You ever see me? Had a great arm—"

"No, but I—"

"Did you ever see *anybody*? You keep sayin' no, no no all the time—" He looked at the ground and muttered, "Never saw Smokey Joe and says he played ball—I ask you . . ."

Thomas felt Coco Grimes had taken a dislike to him, only he didn't know why. He had traveled all this way to meet practically a *legend*, and now somehow had gotten the legend mad at him.

"When did Smokey Joe Williams play, do you know, Mrs. Grimes?" Thomas kept his voice low, hoping the old man, who was holding the glass of lemonade to his lips with a trembling hand, wouldn't hear.

"Before the war. First World War," she added, smiling. "He won his forty-one games in 1914."

"Holy *cow*!"

She got up and smiled at Thomas. "I have a dozen things to do. You're doing fine."

Thomas looked after her pleadingly, wishing she'd stay, but she didn't seem to notice. Or, maybe he thought it was that they appreciated having someone use up part of old Mr. Grimes's time.

Thomas drank thirstily, and gave up the idea of asking Coco about Dave Barnhill or Jimmy Crutchfield, two guys he'd taken a fancy to, reading about them. Better just to listen.

"Called him Cyclone, we did," Mr. Grimes was going on excitedly about some player. "And how about Bullet Rogan, eh? eh? Throw a porkchop past a wolf, Bullet could. All you ever hear about is Satchel Paige. Satch, Satch, nobody ever threw a ball but Satch! Not that he wasn't good, mind. *And* he didn't play no towns where they wouldn't let him sit down at the table an' eat. No back door brown-paper bags for *him*, no sir. We was proud of him for that. But the most of us—we just took what they made us take." He shook his head and blew out a long whistling breath. "Like Gene Benson usta say, 'Wasn't for bad luck we'd wouldn't have no luck at all . . .'"

"So then why," Thomas began again, "did you—why did you put up with it? I mean, why *play*, if you felt that way? I mean, if things were that awful . . ."

Suddenly the pepper seemed to leave Coco Grimes. He seemed to crumple in his chair.

"Not so smart, after all," he said hoarsely. "Well, I'll tell you why, since you can't figger it out for yerself. We played because it was what we loved. We'da played, like Willie Mays's boy, Willie, said, for nothin'. Just to play the game, that's what counted. Go away. I don't want t'talk no more."

Thomas just sat there, feeling miserable, not knowing what to do. A fly landed on the table, took a drink from a drop of spilled lemonade then began to wash its face, just like a cat. Thomas watched it.

"Didn't I tell you to skedaddle!"

"Mr. Grimes. Coco, sir—"

The old man waved his good hand dismissively, and Thomas got to his feet. He trudged to the house, where he found Joe Grimes in the kitchen, repairing a cabinet.

"Finished already?" he asked, sitting back on his heels.

Thomas, blinking back tears, said, "I got him mad. Or sad. I hurt his feelings, Mr. Grimes, and I feel awful about it."

"Oh, now—son. Don't take it to heart. I told you he gets crotchety."

"He wasn't crotchety. He was hurt. I kept getting mixed up about when we were talking about. I couldn't understand him all the time, and I made him feel bad." Thomas slumped to a chair. "I'm awful sorry."

Joe Grimes stood and put an arm over Thomas's shoulder. "See here, Tom—you're a boy and he's an old man and your worlds are so far apart that understanding would be a—an absolute miracle. You can't blame yourself because a miracle didn't happen."

"I guess," Thomas said with a sigh. "Mr. McCallam said your grandfather had a cup of coffee with some team in the Majors, after they got integrated. But *he* says he caught for the Indians—"

"Tom. He never did that. He did know Larry Doby, who was a heck of a nice guy, and when Larry got into organized ball, pretty late at that, with Cleveland, he invited Gramps up for a game, and took him to the locker room to meet the other fellows. Somehow in Gramps's head he's got the idea he caught for them. No harm in that."

"No. I guess not." Thomas stood. "I better get back to the motel, Mr. Grimes. I'm going to the raree this afternoon."

"Tom, before you go, do something for me, will you? And for Gramps. Go on out there and say good-bye to him, tell him how much you enjoyed your talk."

"But he told me to go away. I mean, he really *told* me."

"Trust me, Tom. His memory is great for the days of—of Josh Gibson and Bullet Rogan. The Negro Leagues," Joe Grimes said, shrugging. "But for what happened twenty minutes ago, his memory isn't even there a lot of the time. Go back out there and try."

"Okay, if you say so," Thomas said, sure it was going to be a mistake.

He went again down the back steps, walked across the yard to where the old catcher/infielder/outfielder sat in his wheelchair under the live oak tree, staring at a squirrel.

"Coco?" he said.

Coco Grimes looked up and smiled. "Hey, hey! Whatcha know! It's Tom, right? Seen any good games lately? How you been, anyways?"

"I been just fine," Thomas said, halfway

between a laugh and a cry. "Just fine, Coco. I loved—talking with you."

"Likewise, son. Likewise. You come see me again, sure?"

"Sure, Coco. I sure would like to do that."

Shakily, Coco picked up his glass of lemonade. "Here's to olden days—right, Joe?"

Thomas didn't mind at all being called Joe. He liked it. Taking up his glass, he said, "To olden days, Coco!"

"Good, good," said the old man. He looked at the squirrel again. "What do you think that there cat's up to?" he asked, and closed his eyes.

## Chapter FIVE

**A**t La Casa de Ladra, Aunt Linzy was waiting for him on the portico of the main building.

"Ah," she said. "There you are. Was it a successful interview?"

"I don't know."

"Oh?"

"He's practically a *century* old, Aunt Linzy, and it was like we were trying to talk to each other clear across the whole hundred years."

"Goodness," she said. "That's very well put, Thomas."

"It is?" he said, pleased.

"Something that you certainly should say, if you write it up for your school paper. I was thinking—wouldn't it be interesting if one day you turned out to be a writer."

Thomas thought that'd be interesting, all right. A person could just stay home and make up stories and not have to work at all. Or he could be a sportswriter and get into games free, and know all the players . . .

"Do you want to tell me about it?" his great-aunt asked.

Thomas screwed up his face, trying to re-capture his hour with Coco Grimes.

"Well," he said, "it started okay and ended okay and in between it was neat a lot of the time. But he gets awfully mixed up—like half the time he thought I'd seen these old-timers that've been dead ages ago and that mixed me up and then he got mad and told me to go away, but then Joe, his grandson, asked me to go back out and I did and he didn't even re-member he'd got mad. I mean, angry." He shook his head. "It was pretty confusing, Aunt Linzy."

"Well, you tried. Best remember the good parts. In any case, write about it in your jour-nal while it's still fresh in your mind."

"Yeah. Yeah, I'll do it, as soon as we get back from the raree."

"Are you ready to go now?"

"I sure am."

"It's some distance away, so we'll take my car."

"Great. Let's go."

"Here's five dollars your grandfather left for you, in case you want to buy something."

"Thanks. Maybe I will."

"Remember when we went to the planetarium in Bradenton, to see the Voyager II show?" Thomas asked Aunt Linzy as they drove toward the center of town.

"Of course I do."

"That was fun."

"It certainly was."

Thomas nodded. It was odd—he could remember how much he'd resented Aunt Linzy, even for a while disliked her—but couldn't *feel* that feeling anymore. He still wouldn't want her living with him and Grandfather, but it was nice being with her like this, especially when she didn't try to boss him, which she hardly had done at all, so far.

As they approached the fair grounds, the raree exploded in a racket of music contending against announcements broadcast over the loud, crackly P.A. system. Aunt Linzy parked the car and they walked into a melee of strolling bongo bands and past little stages, where country music singers played their guitars. Jugglers ambled along, keeping impossible numbers of balls aloft, and acrobats twirled and somersaulted through the crowds, turned cartwheels and backflips. On other small elevated stages dancers moved to the music of flutes and recorders. Contortionists twisted atop barrels. On a scrap of Oriental carpet, a skinny mime in a black and silver body suit enacted a silent drama. Past him came a llama wearing a flowered straw hat, stepping daintily through the mob as she pulled a beribboned buggy with a bejeweled poodle reclining in it. Their owner, in a serape, walked beside them, holding a leash of gilt links. An enormous two-man green dragon, scarlet tongued, golden horned, hung all over with golden fringe, lumbered along spouting red smoke, its great tail trundling behind it on a low wagon.

All these activities and sounds rang, sang, jangled over the intertwingling voices of many hundreds, maybe thousands, of browsers.

Thomas watched them move in all directions, carrying toys, balloons, books they'd purchased in a place called "Children's Alley," where writers were sitting with their books piled about them, hoping to sign and sell some. Nearby, in the storytelling booth, he heard a woman reading aloud about Pinocchio.

And everywhere there were uniformed security guards speaking importantly into walkie-talkies as their eyes swept the crowds.

But what Thomas especially noticed was the many tents where ethnic foods, heavy with rich spicy aromas, were being prepared.

"Aunt Linzy," he said. "Do you think . . . you see . . . I haven't had anything to eat since practically dawn, and . . ."

"Well, then . . . what do you want?"

"How about—about—I can't *decide*. It all smells so good!"

Just then a vendor, dressed like Simple Simon, came by with a tray of hot pizzas held high. Thomas sniffed and succumbed. "One of those, Aunt Linzy?" he asked, adding hopefully, "and a Coke?"

Grandfather didn't hold with soft drinks, except at ballgames.

But his aunt said, "Of course. You there, Simon! We'll have two of your best pizzas, please. Let's see, Thomas. There are some with pepperoni, some with anchovies, and sausage—"

"Cheese and pepperoni and sausage," Thomas said eagerly.

"Good. I'll have one without sausage, please."

Aunt Linzy paid for two medium pizzas and led the way to a table where several other people were already eating. She dispatched Thomas to a booth for Cokes, and then while they ate, another vendor passed with a trayful of pastries, and they added some of those to their lunch.

At length, Thomas sat back and sighed. "Boy. That was good. Thanks."

"Do you want ice cream?"

"I guess not yet. Maybe after a while. What'll we do now?"

"Walk about. Gaze at things. Let ourselves be astonished. Oh, look, Thomas! There's a beautiful boa constrictor over there! People are getting to hold it!"

Thomas stared at his aunt with admiration. "You gonna do that?" he asked. "Hold that snake?"

"Oh, my goodness, yes. I consider the serpent one of nature's adornments."

They had to wait while a little girl held the coiling creature, putting her cheek to its scales with an expression of bliss.

"It's so *smooth*," she said to her mother, who looked on, bravely not commenting.

Aunt Linzy's turn came next and she politely offered Thomas first dibs.

"Oh thanks, no, Aunt Linzy. You go ahead. I'll watch."

Tenderly, Aunt Linzy accepted the great creature from its owner and let it twine about her upper body, even her neck. Its slender forked tongue flickered in and out as it turned its head from side to side, seeming to take an interest in its surroundings.

"Really, just like velvet," his aunt said. "Sure you don't want to—"

"No, no," Thomas said, backing away slightly. "He's a nice-looking snake, but I'd just as soon not—" He broke off. Over the P.A.

system came an announcement.

"Attention, folks! The Giant Jigsaw Puzzle Contest is about to begin! Hurry to Alley 18 and test your skill!"

Aunt Linzy was alert as a racer hearing the starting pistol. "Thomas," she said hurriedly, "would it be all right with you if—"

"Sure thing, Aunt Linzy. I think Alley 18 is over back where we came from, near the book people."

Handing over the snake to the next person in line, they raced to a blue-striped tent, where, on a huge table, a jumble of jigsaw pieces was piled. Aunt Linzy was the first person to get her chance to win a prize. Right behind her several other contestants lined up. Each had fifteen minutes to work it out, and Thomas saw right away that his great-aunt wasn't going to have any trouble. The puzzle was one with a picture, and the picture was on an easel right there to look at. He bet his aunt hadn't done a puzzle with a picture since she was his age.

"I'll walk around," he said, "and come back in fifteen minutes, okay?"

Aunt Linzy, already seated and at work, nodded but didn't speak.

Thomas went back to watch the black and silver mime. He was a dark-skinned, very thin, tall man who turned and twisted, revolved and dipped, lifted one leg high, then the other, then an arm, then both arms with his hands flattened skyward. He turned his masked head slowly from side to side, then leaned over so that he was like a great hairpin, took a silver flute from a little case at his feet, straightened and began to play. People who had been going past stopped to listen. Then a little gasp of joy went round as from a tree overhead a mockingbird began to sing along with the flute, following every clear note. For the briefest second, the mime looked as astonished as his audience, but then played on, impassive as if it were part of his plan. For a few minutes he and the bird accompanied each other and then the bird flew away. The mime put his flute away and flowed into the crowd.

Thomas walked on, thinking that what he'd just seen, and heard, was something he'd remember forever. When he was very very old, he decided, even if he lived to be as old as Coco Grimes, he'd still remember that black and silver man and the bird, the two of them making music together like that.

But somehow he didn't think he'd tell anyone about it. Well, maybe, someday, he'd tell his grandfather what it had been like.

But not yet.

Arriving back at the Giant Jigsaw Puzzle tent, Thomas saw that Aunt Linzy had, indeed, won the prize, a huge stuffed crocodile. His aunt looked a bit wry, holding it happily but barely able to get her arms around it.

Thomas laughed. "What'll you do with it, Aunt Linzy?"

"Do you want it?"

"Nope."

"Then I'll save it till Christmas, and give it to the Salvation Army."

"That's a good idea. How long did it take you to do the puzzle?"

"Four minutes, twenty seconds—a record,

I'm told. What have you done with yourself? I see you bought a book."

"About the planets. I figure I'd like to know some more about them, and the constellations."

"Good." His aunt moved her shoulders back. "Dear, do you want to see anything more? If not, my back is beginning to ache, and . . ."

"No. That's okay. I've had a great time, but we can go home now if you want."

They got ice cream cones and ate them on their way to the car.

It was only when he was back in his and Grandfather's cabin that he realized he'd called this place "home."

He sat at the desk and got his journal out.

*Maybe home is where you happen to be?* he wrote, and then, *No, that's not so. It's just that I'm feeling comfortable here and I've had a good time. But home is where Ringo and Donny are, where*

*Grandfather and I* live, *on the Gulf of Mexico, in our* own house.

The next day, after lunch, Grandfather and Thomas started the trip home.

"Were you sorry not to catch a marlin, Grandfather?" Thomas asked after a few miles.

"Not really. The captain got one on his line. It was a beautiful thing, leaping and flashing in the sunlight, and it put up such a fight. I was glad when it threw the hook and sped away like a surfer to its own world."

"I bet the captain wasn't glad."

"Actually, he didn't seem to mind, as long as we didn't. I just liked being out on the water. There were porpoises everywhere, Thomas. They swam along beside the boat, leaping and singing—"

"You could hear them, all right?"

"Oh yes."

He and Thomas had often heard the porpoises singing, but it was not something you ever tired of, or even got used to.

For a while neither Grandfather or Thomas spoke. Thomas just sat back and listened to the soft hum of the motor. He thought about the weekend.

"I'd sort of like to go back one day, to visit them," Thomas said suddenly.

"Well, I can't always be asking Cal for the loan of a car, you know."

"Yup. I know. Anyway, I'm glad we did go."

"So am I. Are you going to tell me about your visit with Coco Grimes?"

"Sometime, Grandfather. I gotta—think about it first. Maybe I'll write it, like Aunt Linzy says I should, and you can read what I write."

"Fine, if that's how you want it."

Another long pause and then Thomas said, "Do you think that lady cop, Pollyanna Welles, is gone on Mr. McCallam?"

"Thomas! You do *not* say 'lady cop.' You say 'policewoman.'" Grandfather frowned and scratched his beard. "Or maybe you say 'Officer Welles.' And I wouldn't have a notion of whether she's 'gone on' him. Certainly nothing

Milo said would indicate it."

"I just wondered."

"Wonder away," said Grandfather, leaning forward as he prepared to change lanes.

Dark was gathering when they pulled into their driveway.

Thomas looked at their small house, at the flower borders, the freshly planted vegetable garden, at the birdbath where a grackle was having a final splash, merrily tossing beads of water, as if he were playing. Sunset, the color of Gatorade, still lingered over the gulf.

"You know something, Grandfather?"

"What's that?"

"I wouldn't mind being sessile, as long as it was here."

"Me, either."

"How about a game of cribbage after dinner?"

"Cribbage would be fine."

Before turning out the light, Thomas took up

his journal and wrote:

*In most ways I'm glad we went. I'll write about Coco Grimes for school. Someday maybe I'll write about that man and the bird. Ringo's glad we're home. So are we.*

*And so to bed.*